We Have a Big, Brown Grizzly Bear

Written By Elizabeth Lammers
Illustrated By Geraldine Tamsi

PublishAmerica
Baltimore

© 2007 by Elizabeth Lammers.
All rights reserved. No part of this book may be reproduced, stored in a retrieval system or transmitted in any form or by any means without the prior written permission of the publishers, except by a reviewer who may quote brief passages in a review to be printed in a newspaper, magazine or journal.

First printing

ISBN: 1-4137-9924-8
PUBLISHED BY PUBLISHAMERICA, LLLP
www.publishamerica.com
Baltimore

Printed in the United States of America

For My Mother

E.L.
To my little cubs: B.A.D, M.K.D., and L.W.D.
And S.N.D, the biggest Grizzly of all.

G.T.
For T and my two little "CATs"—your laughter
is my inspiration.

We have a big, brown grizzly bear.
He's living in our house.

Although he snores ferociously,
He's as quiet as a mouse.

For breakfast he eats honey
And gets his nose stuck in the jar.

For lunch he might have tuna fish
And a chocolate candy bar.

I like to take him for a ride;
I push him on my scooter.

He sits upon the handle bars,
And likes to honk the tooter.

When summer days are quiet,
We lie beneath a tree...

...And watch marshmallow clouds drift by
In shapes of birds and bees.

Beneath a canopy of leaves,
We drift to sleep, it seems.

We grab a hold of kite tails
And soar into our dreams.

Dinner time is quite a treat
For our grizzly bear.

He makes bubbles in his milk
And gets jelly in his hair.

He doesn't like the bath at all.
He really makes a mess.

The water overflows the tub
And splashes mommy's dress.

But at night when we're in bed,
I'm cozy, safe, and warm,

For my grizzly bear hugs me tight,
Protecting me from harm.

The End

Printed in the United States
97660LV00001B